The Summer With Annagale

THE SUMMER WITH ANNAGALE

Colleen Smith

To the Struggle.

Without it this story would not exist.

1

First Sighting

Essentially, this story starts on an eight-hundred-mile road trip, and I remember next to none of it.

I do remember the hot coal of hate sitting in my chest, burning me from the inside out. I remember the piece-of-junk car Mom had bought, with its broken radio. It was stuck on one station: *87.5 The Classics with your pals Polly and Pat!* Their version of "classic" was slow monotone songs from men and women who died long before I was born. I wanted to rip it from the console and throw it out the window. Instead, I stayed hunched in my seat, my hoodie pulled over my head, staring out at the passing scenery. Mom had given up trying to talk to me hours ago, which I was glad—but also pissed about.

We reached Mary's just before sunset; the dying light cast the world in an odd fiery glow, adding to the bizarreness of what my life had become. Mary was Mom's aunt. As the youngest in her family and only twelve years older than Mom, they had always been close. Mary had never married or had children and had offered us a place to stay for as long as we needed.

Mom wouldn't shut up about it.

She praised Mary the whole drive there. I didn't see how it mattered; my world was falling apart—who cared where it happened.

Mom parked the car with a heavy sigh. It'd been years since I'd visited, but the house looked the same: old and sun beaten, the siding a faded pale blue with bleached-white shutters. Below them were thick, overgrown bushes. A sidewalk cut through the lawn from the front door to the street.

Before we could so much as open our doors, Mary ran out of the house, waving and smiling as she made her way to us in loose jeans and bare feet. Opening my car door, she yanked me from the seat and wrapped her arms around my neck in a tight hug.

I hated her.

"My lovelies, welcome! I'm so excited to have you." Resting

her hands on my shoulders she looked into my face. I towered over her by a few inches. "Look at you! You were what, ten when I last saw you? Now you're practically a man." She gave my shoulders a quick squeeze, then moved to Mom and wrapped her in her own tight hug.

Stepping away, I surveyed the landscape. Across the street was an open field of small hills plastered in tall grass, beyond which I could just make out the ocean. This was a small town where people traveled to get away for a relaxing weekend. I only felt oppressed, like the sky was pressing in, suffocating me.

Mary spoke again, cutting through my darkening thoughts. "Let's get you inside and settled. You've had a long drive."

We didn't have much. Mom and I had two bags each, and mom had packed three boxes of things she couldn't bear to part with; it only took us one trip to bring everything inside.

Mary's house was a mix of dark outdated wood and bright yellow paint. Nothing like our home with its light wood and gray tones. Mary led us upstairs and showed me where I would be sleeping. As soon as she did, I walked in and shut the door behind me. The room sported the yellow paint from the rest of the house, but Mary had obviously tried to decorate it for a teenage boy.

Whatever.

With a few steps I stood at the small window and looked out toward the front lawn; from there I could see more of the ocean and the white-capped waves crashing on the shore.

That was when I saw *her* for the first time.

She rode by on a white bike, long blonde hair streaming behind her. Each handlebar held a giant empty basket.

Huh.

Once she was out of sight, I moved to the twin bed in the corner. I lay down and stared at the ceiling, trying to ignore the silence around me and my wandering thoughts. Instead, I focused on my anger, allowing it to consume me and lull me into a fitful sleep.

****

I didn't wake till morning. With a groan, I remembered where I was. Throwing my pillow over my head, I tried to go back to sleep. Maybe I could sleep through everything?

"Aidan!" Mom's yell was muffled, obviously calling me from downstairs.

I didn't answer and groaned again when I heard the creak of a step. Lying as still as I could, I pretended to be asleep. She knocked, only to open the door a moment later. I felt more than heard her walk in and stand next to the bed. I knew what she was doing—she was staring at me. She'd gotten into doing that often. It was one of her more annoying habits.

Luckily, she didn't try to wake me and eventually left.

I knew I wouldn't fall back asleep, but I spent the next hour trying. Having to pee was what finally got me up. I remembered where the bathroom was from years ago. Keeping my eyes averted from my reflection, I did my business, then reluctantly moved to the stairs. Now with my bladder satisfied, my stomach made it clear it had been neglected for long enough. However, I only made it down a few steps before Mary's voice drifted up to me.

"Staci, none of this is your fault. None of it. You tried. Chad knew what he was doing, and he knew it was wrong."

At the mention of my dad's name, I turned around and went back to the room. My stomach would have to suffer.

Everyone said I looked like him.

I hated that.

****

No more than half an hour passed before Mom came looking for me again. This time she had a plate of eggs, bacon, and toast.

"Hungry?"

I sat slumped on the bed, doing nothing, and trying not to think. Before I even shrugged, she handed me the plate and sat down.

Looking around, she smiled. "I think this will be good for us."

I didn't respond. What the hell was that supposed to mean?

"Aidan, we haven't really talked in a while . . ." She left the sentence open-ended, as though waiting for me to confirm what she was saying.

Quickly I stood, not caring I had only taken a few bites of food. "Well, why start now?" I threw all the bitterness and sarcasm I could muster into those four small words.

"Aidan!"

I was already out the door and down the stairs. Ignoring Mary, I left the house as quick as I could. I didn't stop until I was across the street and halfway down the small hill toward the beach. A handful of people milled around on the sandy shore. I plopped down among the weeds; I had no desire to meet anyone, especially not in a small town like this.

I sat, people-watching and fuming for the rest of the morning and the afternoon. My stomach went from growling to empty and hollow, but I couldn't go back inside—I didn't want to see Mom or Mary.

I didn't want to see anyone.

"Heads up!"

I turned in time to see a paper-wrapped *something* come flying toward my face. I caught it before it hit me and realized it was a sandwich. Mary stood only a few feet above me, as if my thoughts had made her materialize. I looked from the sandwich to her and back, waiting for the lecture. All she did was catch my eye and throw me another sandwich. With the smallest of smiles, she turned and walked back toward the house.

That was unexpected.

But I had never been happier to see roast beef. I told myself I would thank her later as I hungrily ripped the paper open and dug in.

After eating, I lay down on the soft sand, the sun warm against my skin, and fell into yet another fitful sleep. I wasn't sure what woke me, but more bodily functions urged me to get up and return to the house.

That was when I saw *her* for the second time. She was headed in the opposite direction from the night before, riding the same bike. She wore overalls, and her hair was in two long braids. She looked to be around my age, perhaps a year younger. The handlebars held the same baskets but were now weighed down with bright yellow flowers.

What was she doing with them?

Why did I care?

Still, I watched as she pedaled down the road until she took a turn and vanished from sight.

2

Cemetery

I watched for and observed her during the next few days; there honestly wasn't much else to do. Almost every day she'd ride by. Same bike and same two baskets overflowing with yellow flowers. She intrigued me, and I found myself growing more curious each day. I hadn't cared about anything in a long time. But I was drawn to her, and this mystery was more interesting than staring at the ocean every day.

On the sixth day, I decided to follow.

She was already well ahead of me, only feet away from making the turn that took her out of sight, when I broke into a run.

I'd been on the track team all through junior high and most of high school, and I'd been decent—more than decent—I'd been *good*. It had, however, been months since I had so much as done a brisk walk. It felt good to push my body, but I could feel the results of spending months sitting around. My lungs and calves burned as I turned the corner a few minutes after she had. Just as I did, I saw her up ahead, turning right. I pushed myself harder, not wanting to lose her.

When I finally reached the next turn, I stopped dead in my tracks.

Before me was a sprawling cemetery. It was surrounded by foreboding trees and had come out of nowhere. Heavy, thick iron gates stood open, fencing in the smaller trees, dirt walkways, and tombstones of various shapes, sizes, and conditions. I looked around but couldn't see her. With slow steps, I walked past the gates, a stillness spreading through and around me. I picked the closest trail and followed its path.

It took almost five minutes to find her. The cemetery was huge, surprising for such a small town. The ground rose in small irregular hills with paths leading off in various directions. I spotted bright yellow flowers atop each tombstone before I spotted her. She moved from one grave to the next, gingerly placing a flower on each one.

This was where she went every day? My chest tightened, as a

mix of emotions rose inside. I couldn't explain what I was feeling even if I wanted to.

Slower still, I walked to where she was. As I got close, she glanced up and offered a small smile before returning to her task.

I felt like an idiot, but the words came out, loud and abrupt. "What are you doing?"

She glanced back at me, her eyebrows raised. As she looked around at the tombstones she had already finished, her smile broadened, and she spoke. "Painting the world with a little bit of color." She moved to the next stone and placed a flower on top.

"Why? Are you dying or something?" I said it in jest. I couldn't think of another reason why someone would come to a cemetery every day.

I also couldn't think of a reason why I cared, but here we were.

She froze for a few seconds before slowly turning to face me. It felt like hours before she finally said something—and all the while I stood there, awkwardly, waiting.

She took another flower from her basket. Instead of placing it on the next tombstone, she took a step closer and handed it to me. With her smile still in place, she answered, "We're all dying, aren't we?" Her face was open and bright, her smile genuine.

We stared at each other for another long moment. I didn't know how to respond. Was I right? Was she dying? Had I just been an insensitive jerk? I opened my mouth to say something, but no words came.

She stared at me, waiting a few more minutes. With a larger smile, she turned back to her basket and continued down the row. I was frozen to the spot, staring between her and the flower. Finally, I turned and headed back the way I'd come.

I spent the rest of the evening in my room, studying the flower's yellow petals. The encounter had been strange—but there had been something about her eyes, about her smile, something about her flowers. Something I couldn't describe. I fell asleep quickly with a plan to see her again the next day.

****

Seeing the flower in the morning buoyed my mood like nothing else had in a long time. I even made my way downstairs for breakfast. I knew Mom and Mary were both surprised to see me. Luckily, they didn't make a big deal of it.

I surprised them more when I voluntarily spoke while eating my omelet. "Do you know everyone in town?" I addressed Mary across the table. They were the first words I had spoken to her.

She took them in stride.

"No." She chuckled at my ignorance. "This town may be small, but it's not *that* small. I do know most of my neighbors though." She paused, waiting for me to continue, but I regretted asking as soon as I opened my mouth.

What was I supposed to say next? Do you know the blonde girl who puts flowers on gravestones? Instead, I shrugged and focused on my breakfast. I knew they were staring at each other, wondering what was wrong with me. Again, they didn't say anything.

After breakfast, I went back to the hill overlooking the ocean. Something was stirring in my chest, an emotion other than anger. It felt odd after so long. I wasn't sure I trusted it; I also wasn't sure I wanted it to leave. I watched the road, waiting for her to ride by, the flower she had given me cradled in my hand. I didn't have a plan on what I was going to do. Stop her? Follow her? I didn't know, but I watched and waited.

Somehow, I had missed her so when six o'clock hit and I had yet to see her pedaling by, I decided to go to the cemetery and check there. I walked this time and, despite myself, enjoyed the salty ocean air. As I made the turn past the gates, I was surprised to see more people than the day before. I gave them a wide berth and stayed along the exterior of the yard, heading to where I'd last seen her. The lawns were dotted with stone and yellow flowers. I continued walking. She'd had a lot of flowers yesterday, but not enough to cover the whole cemetery—I figured I would eventually hit a section where there were no flowers, and I hoped she would be there.

I didn't make it that far.

As I crested a hill, I came upon a funeral. Thirty or so people, all dressed in black. A woman sat on a folding chair facing a gaping hole in the earth, sobbing.

I shouldn't have been shocked; I was, after all, in a cemetery. But seeing the results of death so close took not only my breath away but also squashed the flutter of emotion that had started to bloom. My anger came back in a flash. I dropped the flower, crushing it under my foot as I turned and stalked back home.

There was no goodness in this world. Only pain and loss.

The woman's cries followed me home and haunted my dreams.

3

Confrontation

The next few days passed excruciatingly slow. I was worse off than I had been before allowing myself to feel. It felt like the world was mocking and punishing me for believing in anything good. I stayed in my room as much as possible, alone with my thoughts, my anger, and my annoyance. I snapped at both Mom and Mary, waiting for the inevitable moment I'd go too far, and they'd yell back at me. But my only punishment had been the tears Mom tried to hide after asking if I wanted to come down and watch a movie.

It was the day after that that I saw *her* again riding by, as if nothing had happened, as if she hadn't lifted my spirits only to send them crashing down again. Before I thought anything through, I ran down the stairs, out the door, and along the road.

It took me longer to find her this time; she was toward the far back of the cemetery with one of her ridiculously large baskets in the crook of her arm, placing one flower down after another.

Before I reached her, I yelled across the twenty or so yards separating us, "Why do you do that? It's not helping! People still die, people still leave . . . It doesn't change anything! Flowers do nothing." I hated those flowers; I wanted to crumple them and stomp on them until they were only dust beneath my feet.

She straightened and looked at me, tilting her head to the side before glancing around at her handiwork, then back at me.

I was fuming. I wanted her to yell at me, tell me I was being a jerk, that I was acting crazy. Instead, she put the basket down and closed the distance between us. Her bright blue eyes watched me. My muscles and nerves taut as I waited for her response. Would she give me more than a few random words this time?

"Do you want to go sit on the beach?"

I drew back with surprise, that was not what I had expected. "What?"

"The beach?" She pointed to her left at a small opening in the iron fence. "Do you want to go?"

When I didn't respond, she grabbed my hand and pulled me across the lawn and through the opening. We passed through the trees and ventured across a dirt road and down a small sandy hill leading to a semi-secluded beach. Stopping, she closed her eyes, tilted her head back, and took a deep breath. Then she pulled me a few more steps until we were just before the tide line. Sitting, she tugged me down with her.

For five minutes we sat there, doing nothing. They were some of the most awkward minutes I had ever experienced. All I could do was stare at her, waiting for her to do or say something.

Finally, she turned to me with a smile on her face. "Do you know what scientists say about moving water?" She wasn't fazed when I didn't respond, and simply continued talking. "It's full of negative ions, which at first sounds like a bad thing, but when we soak them into our bodies, they produce chemicals that make us happy." She breathed deeply, holding her breath for a few seconds. Letting the air go, she added, "Can you feel the tide taking your negative thoughts and worries away? Taking them to its depths and leaving you with hope and happiness?"

Realization dawned. This girl was nuts. One of those voodoo types.

What had I gotten myself into? Before she started to chant or dance around, I quickly stood, brushing the sand from my jeans. "Whatever."

I began backtracking our steps through the soft sand and made it all the way to the road before I heard her shout, "Wait! We should be friends!"

That stopped me.

I turned around and stared at her incredulously. "What?"

Her shoulder rose and fell in a shrug. "We should be friends, don't you think?"

As I stared at her, a myriad of emotions ran through me. I felt stupid, stupid for following her to this beach, stupid for believing—I don't know—that she held some sort of answer. I should turn and run, and yet I found myself throwing my arms into the air as I yelled back, "I guess."

I started walking again, needing to get away from her before I did anything else stupid. Before I was out of earshot, she yelled out one last time. This time I didn't stop.

"My name's Annagale!"

4

Lunch Date

She was crazy, and I didn't need more crazy in my life. I didn't need her or her flowers or her stupid negative ions.

I didn't need *anyone*.

Whatever.

I wasn't going back.

Annagale. What kind of name was that?

I rolled over and buried my face in my pillow, breathing in the smell of salt and detergent; someone had washed my bedding.

Why was I wasting my time thinking about her? I was just starved for human interaction; she was the only person I had met here and the only one around my age I'd seen. I was, in fact, getting sick of my own company. Pulling myself from the bed I moved to the door but hesitated before twisting the knob.

Talking with Mom or Mary was not really what I wanted to do. But I needed to be around someone other than myself. There was a time I'd liked being around people.

Before I could talk myself out of it, I pushed the door open and made my way downstairs. Mary stood at the stove, stirring a large pot of something that filled the room with a warm and savory aroma, while Mom sat a few steps away in the back room at a computer. I was surprised it still worked; it was clearly from the '90s with its large off-white monitor and small screen.

Mom jumped up when she saw me. "Aidan! Are you hungry? Can I get you something?"

Her concern annoyed me. She was always looking at me as if at any moment I would break into a million pieces. "I'm fine."

She winced at my tone. Perhaps I had said it a bit harshly. But she never listened. How many times did I have to say I was fine?

Mary spoke up. "Where did you go off to in such a hurry yesterday?"

So, they had seen me tear out of the house like a maniac. *Great.*

"Running." It wasn't really a lie, and they didn't need to know the truth. Still, I didn't meet their eyes. Instead, I looked around the small room. Like the rest of the house, it was bright but dated. It had a welcoming and homey feeling.

"You went running?" Mom sounded like she was about to cry.

"It's not a big deal." I quickly changed the subject. "Is there anything to do in this town?"

"Loads." Mary continued stirring whatever she had in her pot.

"Like?" I tried to suppress my annoyance; I doubt I hid it well.

I felt Mary turn to face me, but I didn't turn to face her. Instead, I looked at the various knickknacks and pictures she had on her mantel. She had photographs of herself and others smiling from frames of various sizes and colors. The pictures were taken from all over the world. They were intermixed with small replicas of the Eiffel Tower, the Pyramids, The Great Wall of China, and numerous beads and necklaces. It looked like she had been everywhere and done everything. *Huh*. Mary might be kind of cool.

Mary spoke behind me. "Your mother is helping me with my garden. We need a strong man to carry the soil we're gonna buy."

I groaned. That was not what I had in mind, but I didn't press it, what was my alternative? Go back to the room and continue thinking about *her?*

****

An hour later, we piled into Mary's Jeep and drove into town—which literally only consisted of Main Street. Mary drove straight to a large building called The Garden. It was full of various plants, flowers, and bright, smiling people eager to meet the newcomers.

I had done a decent job staying away from almost all prying eyes, and so apparently had Mom. She looked almost as uncomfortable as I felt. Mary ended up answering all the questions thrown our way with vague responses and turning the conversation back to the inquirer. Five thirty-pound bags of soil and about a million potted plants later, we were finally done. The only thing not considered was how we would get back with a full car. Mom was saying how she could stay behind while Mary and I unloaded, when a voice called out from down the street.

"Hey!"

Somehow knowing the voice was for us, we turned to look. Running toward us, blonde hair loose and trailing behind her, was Annagale. She stopped before me; mouth turned up into a smile. "I knew today was going to be a good day!"

I could feel Mom's and Mary's eyes on me, but there was no way I was going to tell them who she was or how I knew her.

Her eyes, however, drifted toward them. "Hi, I'm Annagale."

They said their hellos, and we stood waiting for something—most likely for me to speak, which I wasn't going to do.

Annagale, unfazed, turned back to Mom and Mary. "Would it be okay if I stole him for a bit?"

"Aidan, you know . . . Annagale?" Mom tried hard to hide her surprise.

"Aidan? That's your name?" Annagale looked me over and nodded. "I like it."

I answered Mom's question. "Umm, kind of."

Mary gave a nod, adding, "Well, that would solve our space issue."

"I guess," Mom said. "If you want to?"

Annagale grabbed my arm. "We'll go to lunch. I know the perfect spot."

I nodded. "Sure." Even though I knew she was nuts and had spent a good part of the last twenty-four hours trying not to think about her, I wasn't disappointed at seeing her again. I really must have been starved for company.

"Be back before it gets too late." Mom said as she kept trying to catch my eye. I had become a master at eye aversion and was using every trick I knew in that moment. Finally, Mary got her into the Jeep, and they drove away, leaving me and Annagale alone.

"Come on, Aidan!" Annagale pulled me down the street.

I couldn't deny that things seemed brighter around her—she was like a star pulling everything into her orbit. She seemed to know everyone in town. Well, she waved and smiled at everyone, at least. I watched the people as we continued—their faces were lighter, their smiles genuine. Annagale seemed to leave a spot better by being there.

Anyone would be hard-pressed not to be fascinated by it. Annagale was a mystery, and that, I decided, was why I'd kept thinking of her.

We stopped at a diner, which looked like it was from the 1950s. We were seated next to a large window, and Annagale disappeared behind a laminated menu. "They have everything here, and it's all delicious."

The diner was slow, and within minutes the waiter came to take our orders.

Annagale ordered with her customary smile. "I would like the Classic hamburger, your sweet potato fries, a Caesar salad, a strawberry lemonade, and a chocolate shake."

The waiter turned to me, and I realized I had no idea what was on the menu. Mine lay in front of me untouched. I had been too busy studying Annagale. "Umm, I'll have the same."

The waiter took our order and left us staring at each other.

Annagale didn't let the silence last long. "This is my favorite part of a relationship! The beginning. We know nothing about each other, which makes everything so exciting. Favorite color, food, movie . . . It all gives us a small glimpse into the other person's soul, and I think that's thrilling!"

Her smile and energy were hard to ignore. I had spent months not caring about anything, pushing down all emotion until it was hard for me to remember how to care or even remember who I used to be. Her smile seemed to unlock a part of me; I wasn't sure what would come out, but I let it open slightly.

I leaned across the table. "I'm guessing you're the type of person to eat dessert first. You only live once and all that?" I raised an eyebrow, waiting for her response. The food came before she answered.

Once everything was on the table, she looked at me, her eyes shining with merriment. "I like to think any moment could be a moment, you know? The type of moment that lingers with you for years. A moment that becomes a cherished and sweet memory. Eating is something we do out of necessity and habit, but what if having lunch could be a moment? How exhilarating! I like to decide what taste I want on my tongue last. I take a bite of everything and then decide in what order I'll eat."

Picking up the hamburger, she took a bite and closed her eyes. She did that with everything she ordered. Once done she nodded as if confirming with herself. "Hamburger, salad, fries, drink, and then shake." She gestured to my food. "You try."

I did as she instructed, bemused but willing to play along. I had never thought much about food. I knew what I liked, but I had never separated and judged the food like this before. I started with the hamburger as well. The meat was well seasoned, the tomato sweet, and the lettuce crisp. Some type of sauce added a bit of spice. It was, in all honesty, one of the best hamburgers I'd had. The fries were next. They were coated with a salt blend that mixed nicely with the sweetness of the sweet potato. The Caesar salad surprised me with its sharp tang. I had never been a fan, but I could tell this dressing was handmade, and it was *delicious*. The lemonade was refreshing, just too sweet, and the shake tasted like real chocolate, not the crappy syrup so many places used.

Annagale waited patiently, her eyes bright with anticipation. "Hamburger and fries together—how can you eat them separately? Chocolate shake and then the salad. The drink is too sweet for me."

Annagale leaned across the table. "Isn't it remarkable that this—right now—could be a moment? That from here on out, every time we eat a hamburger, we're transported back to this moment in time?"

Her face was so full of contentment and happiness, I wanted to believe whatever she said. She raised her hamburger in mock cheers and took another bite. A comfortable silence fell between us as we enjoyed our food.

It *really* was good food.

As I finished off my salad, I couldn't stop myself from asking the question that wouldn't leave my mind. "So, are you . . . are you dying?"

Taking a sip of lemonade, she tilted her head. "You seem rather fascinated with death. Why?"

I chuckled dryly. "You make me sound morbid." I had been dragged to enough teen rom-coms to know she fit the bill for the soon-to-be-dying character. Plus, she frequented cemeteries— often. Who does *that*?

"You know that was practically the first thing you ever asked me?"

I chuckled again. Perhaps I was a bit morbid, but it didn't go unnoticed that she had avoided the question.

By the time we ordered another round of chocolate shakes, our conversation had moved on to more pleasant topics. The funny thing is I don't remember what they were.

I do remember how the Caesar salad tasted, how warm the sun felt on my shoulder, and I remember the sound of Annagale's laugh—it was unrestrained and contagious.

Most of all I remember feeling like the old me.

Lunch lasted hours. The owners didn't seem to mind; they seemed almost glad we were there. Afterward, I walked her home to a large white-and-blue house on a hill, its backyard overlooking the ocean. This was the type of house one would expect in a town like this. It screamed beachfront property.

Annagale gave me a tight hug. "I think this friendship is going to work out! Now, follow this road down to Maple, turn right on Cherry Lane, and your aunt's house is down the street."

Apparently, she did know where I lived. I liked the idea that I might have been on her mind as much as she had been on mine. I waited until she closed her front door. Leisurely I made my way back to Mary's. That lunch would definitely fall under the category of a moment.

As soon as I opened the front door, Mom and Mary rushed inside, both wearing garden gloves covered in dirt. "So, who was that?"

I shook my head, but I wasn't as annoyed as I normally would've been. Instead, I smiled and threw my answer over my shoulder as I began climbing the stairs. "A friend."

5

Reality Comes Crashing Back Down

The next day, I made my way over to Annagale's. It was the first day I wanted to wake up early, the first day I didn't find myself hating everything and everyone. I didn't know how she did it; she had brought a part of me back. I wanted—almost needed—to be near her.

About halfway between our houses, we bumped into each other. Laughing at our timing, we exchanged numbers. She told me to change into my swimsuit and meet her at the beach in half an hour. I willingly followed her orders. It was a beautiful day, and people were taking advantage of it; the beach was busy but not uncomfortably crowded. We claimed our spot in the sand, and

Annagale pulled me toward the water. "Come on! Let's get our negative ions on."

The last time I had been to the beach was during a family reunion when I was twelve. My cousins and I had spent the whole day swimming, chasing each other, and building sandcastles. As I got older, the excitement of digging my hands in the dirty sand faded. Without motorized toys like boats and Jet Skis, I never understood how or why adults liked the beach. But Annagale brought back the wonder of it all. We raced in the water, searched for seashells, and yes, even had a sandcastle competition, which I very proudly won.

That wasn't all. While I would have gladly ignored everyone, Annagale invited people in. A few of her friends joined us for a couple of hours before leaving for their summer jobs or vacations. Even people she didn't know were welcomed. The kids from two other groups joined us in building sandcastles, and Annagale talked with everyone we met, asking for their names, how they were doing, and wishing them a fantastic day. It was magic, watching her. I couldn't explain how she did what she did—how she took an everyday moment and made it a memory.

Finally, we ate the lunch Annagale had packed—ham and cheese sandwiches and freshly cut watermelon—and talked as the sun moved across the sky. The beach had quieted down, most of the people having left to find food or entertainment elsewhere.

"I'm just saying, when was the last time an original movie came out? Everything now is a remake, a sequel, or a horror film. What happened to the imagination in Hollywood?"

Annagale laughed. "I'm not denying it! I would rather watch the movies I own, but no matter how large a screen you have or if you have the best surround sound, it's not the same as going to the theater! The smell of popcorn, the slightly sticky floors, the moment when the lights dim, the noise drops, and you get the small flutter of excitement knowing it's about to begin."

"Yeah, after twenty minutes of commercials!"

She slugged my arm with a roll of her eyes.

I grinned. "Can we agree a good movie is a movie you watch over and over again? That no matter how many times you watch it, it draws you back in and you discover new and interesting details?"

"Well, Aidan, you're a bit of a romantic, aren't you?" She reached her hand out, and we shook. "I can agree to that."

It had been a long time since I'd had a good day, but that day and the ones following were some of the best I'd had in months.

If only good things could last.

****

Annagale and I started spending the mornings running on the beach.

It felt good to run again, to stretch my legs and my lungs, to feel my heartbeat rise with each step. To feel the sand and smell the ocean was a welcome bonus. So was having Annagale with me.

She wasn't much of a runner, but she enjoyed pushing herself. I went slowly, knowing she wouldn't be able to go as far or as fast as I could; I had been running for years, after all. There was also the feeling I couldn't shake, that her moments were numbered. We had been running for four days, and she seemed fine. Still, I watched her closely.

After our run, Annagale's parents met us at the beach to pick her up. Apparently, they were going antiquing. They invited me to join, but I declined; the day was too beautiful to be inside looking at people's old junk. I ended up staying at the beach and people-watched for a few hours. When my stomach protested the lack of food, I jogged back to Mary's. As soon as I opened the door, I knew something was wrong. Before I saw Mary's face, before I heard Mom's voice, I felt it—a dark cloud hanging in the air.

Mary was leaning against the wall in the back room, her arms folded, her head bowed. She stared at a spot on the floor, listening to Mom's voice drifting through the backyard's screen door. Her voice was higher than normal; it only ever got like that when she was upset or crying.

I listened closely to what she was saying.

"Chad, you can't do this!"

My stomach and heart plummeted. The bubble of happiness I had found myself in the last few days burst, leaving me cold, angry, and numb.

"What's going on?"

Mary's head jerked up. "Aidan—" She took a step closer. I took a step back.

Mom was now screaming; I couldn't make out what she was saying. What the hell had he done now?

A second later, Mom walked back inside, wiping the tears from her eyes. The second she saw me she stopped in her tracks. "Aidan . . ."

I cut her off with the obvious question. "Was that Dad?"

She wrapped her arms around her waist, as if giving herself a hug. Nodding, she took a deep breath. "He umm, he wanted to talk to you. He. . ." She took another deep breath as my hands clenched into fists. "He wants custody."

My whole body shook.

The anger that had filled me for months flooded back more intensely than ever before. I felt like throwing up.

"What?"

Mom wiped her eyes as more tears fell. "He said he always wanted you to stay with him. He thinks that you should finish high school with your friends. He wants to go to court."

"And you're going to let him do whatever the hell he wants? Like you did with everything else? He hasn't reached out to me once since he left! Screw him—and you."

"Aidan!" Mary's eyes flashed.

"Screw you too!" I was out the door before they could say anything else.

****

I took off running, paying little heed to where I was going. I ran past the cemetery and down the road, straight toward town. I stopped before I got there; I needed to be away from people, not surrounded by them. I turned right and headed for the ocean; I kept my distance from the few people still out. What once had looked like a beautiful day now only reminded me, I had nothing in common with these happy people.

It was almost sunset when I left the beach. I knew where I wanted to go, who I wanted to see. It wasn't because I thought she could make me feel better. No amount of smiles could make me feel better. I was mad, and honestly, my plan was to yell at her. I knocked on the door, unsure if she and her family would be back yet, but her mom answered with a smile. I don't remember what I said, but she willingly led me to the backyard. Annagale sat at a table, canvas, paints, and brushes in front of her.

"Aidan!" Her smile only faltered slightly when she saw my face. Neither of us said anything until her mom had gone back into the house. Annagale tilted her head to the side, watching me, waiting for me to say something. I looked across the yard. The setting sun was lighting the ocean with an orange fire. I hoped it would burn.

Her voice was low when she spoke. "It's beautiful, isn't it?"

I shook my head, my anger growing again. "Life isn't sunsets and rainbows! Life sucks and is full of hate and greed and . . ." I trailed off, not sure how to put my anger into words.

Annagale didn't say anything for a long time. When she did,

her words took me by surprise. "Come paint with me."

I shook my head.

"Come on. I'm painting the sunset. Paint it with me."

She grabbed another canvas and set up a spot for me at the table.

"I don't know how to paint."

"You can't move a brush up and down?" She laughed. "You don't have to paint a masterpiece."

She sat down and picked up her brush. I stood there stubbornly for a few moments but finally took a seat as well. My anger, although still strong, had somewhat faded. I no longer wanted to scream or yell; I wanted to cry.

"I don't know what I'm supposed to do."

"Paint however the sunset makes you feel." She was already fast at work, her brush dipped in paint was gliding along the canvas.

I picked up a brush and started.

****

By the time we were done, the sun had gone down and Annagale's parents had turned on the backyard lights. Annagale moved her chair beside mine and studied my painting. The bottom fourth had the orange and red of the setting sun. The rest was black.

Sunsets aren't magnificent. They're the last bit of hope before the world is unavoidably enveloped in darkness.

Her voice was only a whisper. "It's hauntingly beautiful."

With those words, I broke. In a rush, I told her everything. How my dad had lied and cheated for months with a neighbor. How he had finally broken the news at a family dinner right before my first race of the season. How he had wanted nothing to do with us after that. How he had taken everything, leaving me and my mom without a home or a way to provide for ourselves. How he had called, after five months of no contact, and now wanted custody.

I waited, wondering what Annagale would say. She had the perfect family, the almost perfect life. What would her sunny outlook say to what I had told her?

She didn't say anything.

Her arm wound around my shoulders, as we sat there watching the stars fill the darkening sky.

6

Taste of life Without Annagale

Somehow telling her made things . . . well, not better, but tolerable. The weight that seemed to crush me was lighter. As I stared at my painting—with Annagale's arm still around me—I had an odd and fleeting feeling that things might be okay, that these shattered bits of my life could mend.

Annagale's mom came out a few minutes later, letting me know Mary had called. I knew I had finally crossed the line. I knew Mom would be crying and Mary would be furious. Still, I had been right. Mom let Dad get away with everything. He had taken the house, the cars, everything—all without a fight. Mom said she didn't want to cause more strife. But rolling over didn't bring peace. They had decided everything without my input, making decisions that would affect my life without a second thought of what I wanted. Dad now thought Mom would bend to his every will with a simple phone call. I wasn't so easily bendable.

I declined a ride home, leaving after giving Annagale a long hug and a whispered, "Thank you."

Mary's porch light was on, but the rest of the house was dark. I still expected them to be sitting in the living room, waiting. All I found was a note saying dinner was in the fridge. I should have been hungry, I hadn't eaten in hours, but I wasn't, I was exhausted and getting into bed was all I could do. As soon as my head hit the pillow, I was asleep.

****

When my eyes opened, it was still dark. I turned over to go back to sleep, eager to get as much rest as I could, when I heard a soft tap. Freezing, I listened closely; a few minutes passed, and I heard another tap. Dragging myself out of bed, I moved to the window. It was early morning—sunrise still at least forty-five minutes away. Pushing aside the curtains, I stared out into the darkness, trying to find the source of the sound. Straight below my window, a click of a flashlight illuminated Annagale. She waved me down.

Sleep fled, and I quickly grabbed my jacket, worried something had happened. Annagale met me at the door.

I searched her face. "What's wrong?"

"I thought today would be the perfect day to watch the sunrise."

I stared at her as my heart returned to its normal pace. She wanted to watch the sunrise? My mind returned to my painting and everything it meant. "Yeah, okay."

She placed a hand on my chest, gently pushing me back through the door. "First, leave a note for your mom. We may not be back before she wakes up."

As quickly as I could in the dark house, I left a message and hurried back outside. Annagale led me up the street. The world was quiet around us; it felt eerie yet peaceful.

"Where are we going?"

"Trust me, you'll love it."

We ended up on a hill next to a red-and-white lighthouse. Annagale spread out a blanket, and we sat, listening to the unseen water crash on the shore.

She bumped my shoulder. "Hey."

"Hey."

"How are you?"

I shrugged. "Better, I guess."

She leaned her head on my shoulder, and we watched as the world around us grew light, bit by bit. It was beautiful, watching the sun touch the sea in a pink haze; in one moment the world was black, and the next it was light and bright.

A new day.

A brighter day.

A hopeful day.

"Listen, this seems like the worst time, but . . ." Annagale hesitated, making me look at her. She seemed nervous, uneasy. "We're visiting my grandma for a week. We go every year. I hate to leave now, but my dad got the days off . . ."

I didn't know if it was the hesitation or the fact that she wouldn't look me in the eyes, but my heart skipped a few beats. A strong thought that this was not a visit to her grandma almost overwhelmed me. I wished she would tell me what was wrong with her, but I had my own pains and secrets. I had to trust she would tell me hers in time.

Hopefully in enough time.

She continued, "Will you help me with something?" She stood and faced the road. Next to her bike, which I only now noticed, were two large baskets of small yellow flowers.

****

It was monotonous work, putting a single flower on each grave, but also strangely therapeutic. As we worked, I was again blown away by Annagale. She talked with the mourners and maintenance crew, giving each a smile, a flower, and something else. Something she had given me when we first met.

Hope.

Hope that this life wasn't as crappy as it so often felt. Hope that there was good in this world. And with that, I realized the world wasn't ready to lose her—that *I* wasn't ready. If she was sick, she could be taken at any moment. And if she were taken, the hope and light she brought would be gone. Annagale wouldn't want that. She would want someone to continue her work . . . for me to continue.

She left that afternoon, and my own worries fell to the wayside. I started to plan. I wanted to have something to show her when she returned.

****

I wasn't sure if I avoided them or they avoided me, but I went the whole day without seeing Mom or Mary. Something for which I wasn't going to complain about.

The next morning, I was up early and ready to channel Annagale. First, I jogged back to the cemetery. I had no idea where she got the flowers, but I could find another way to do something, couldn't I? I walked along the tombstones, but all was quiet. Besides helping a maintenance worker pick up some tools he had dropped, there was nothing else to do.

Next, I tried the beach. I easily spotted a family with haggard-looking parents; I could build sandcastles with the kids and give the parents a well-deserved break, but I realized a teenage boy asking to play with kids might come off as creepy. I even tried walking down Main Street, hoping someone with some need would jump out at me. After talking to two different people, and both knowing way more of my life than I was comfortable with, I left.

Annagale made this look effortless—she seamlessly brought the sunlight with her. As I walked back to Mary's, I realized an obvious truth: nothing was working because I was not Annagale.

No one, least of all me, could take her place.

When I reached the house, it was still early afternoon. Tentatively, I opened the door. I knew we would have to talk about dad's phone call and the way I acted, but I wasn't ready yet. The thought of him angered me, and I was sick of being angry and hurt. No one was in the front room or the kitchen. Relieved, I moved toward the stairs, and then I *saw* her.

Mom was sitting on the couch in the back room, her knees pulled up tight against her chest, her arms wrapped around them, hugging herself. Even from here, I could see the tears in her eyes.

She looked so small and fragile.

So human.

The wall I had stubbornly built, a defense against feeling, an excuse that I was the only one suffering, broke. On their own accord, my feet moved toward her.

When she heard me, she jumped up and wiped her cheeks. "Oh, Aidan . . ."

"Do you want to get lunch?" I asked.

Clearly taken aback, she was silent for a few heartbeats. "Sure."

I smiled weakly. "I know the perfect place."

7

Maybe It's a Magical Booth

Mary let us borrow the Jeep, and we drove in an awkward silence to Annagale's diner. In actuality it was called Teddy's, but to me it will always be Annagale's. Strangely enough, we were seated at the same booth Annagale, and I had sat at. Mom and I slid into the red-and-white vinyl seats and took up our menus. I looked over the top of mine at Mom. Annagale had broken down my walls with a simple lunch. Would that work with Mom and me?

Mom looked tired and sad; how had I not realized that before?

I needed to apologize, but I couldn't seem to find the words. We didn't say anything as we ordered and waited for the food.

Even after our orders were delivered, we didn't say anything, but it felt less awkward having something in front of us. The minutes ticked by until Mom chuckled softly, almost humorlessly.

"You know, I used to always make something out of my food before eating it. Nothing big or messy. A word with my peas, an outline in my mashed potatoes. It's stupid, childish . . . It used to make me happy." She absentmindedly moved a crouton around her salad.

There it was again. Human. My mom, like me, was just human.

She stopped fidgeting with the crouton and took a bite of her salad. It was an odd thing to do, playing with your food, but it was harmless and made her happy. Why had she stopped?

I took a deep breath and tried once again to channel Annagale. I rearranged the fries on my plate to look like a rocket ship, the ketchup acting as the fuel. Without saying anything, I slid it across the table. Mom looked startled, then her face spread into a large smile. The sight took me back to almost a year ago. Had it really been that long since I'd seen her smile? With that thought, a lump formed in my throat. I'd been a complete jerk. I may have lost my father, but she had lost her husband.

"I hate him, and I don't want to live with him."

Her eyes flashed to mine. "You shouldn't hate—"

I cut her off. "Mom, I'm not a child. I know what he did. He's a jerk." She sighed, but I continued talking before she could say anything more. "I haven't been the best either. I'm sorry."

"Aidan, you're a good boy. You've had a lot to deal with. I'm sorry for all of it. We've all made mistakes. I don't know what I'm doing. I'm trying to do my best. Honey, you've given up your whole life . . . If you decided to live with your dad, you could finish high school with your friends and at least have some normalcy back."

I wondered if Mom wanted me off her hands; taking care of two people was a lot more work than one. Then I thought back to all the times she watched me sleep, asked me how I was doing— all the small things I'd found annoying had been her trying to make sure I was okay. To remind me I was loved.

"I don't care. I don't want to go back. We can figure this out together. Please, let me help."

She smiled again, tears in her eyes. "I love you, honey."

My throat grew tighter. "I love you too."

She took a fry and thought as she chewed. "Okay, we'll figure things out—together."

Life had been messed up for so long, I'd forgotten what it was like to feel in control. I smiled as well, and we started talking about possibilities.

We also talked about Mary and the other summers Mom had spent with her. We talked about Annagale and what the two of us did. When lunch was over, we ordered pie and continued talking. We hadn't talked in a long time, and although life would never be as it used to, it felt familiar. We realized we weren't going through this alone, and that gave us some long-forgotten courage.

I don't know, maybe it's a magical booth.

8

I'm Not Annagale

Lunch with Mom inspired my second realization of the day: I may not be Annagale but being Aidan might be enough. I didn't have to do what Annagale did, I just had to do *something*.

The next morning, I went downstairs, swallowed my pride, and apologized to Mary.

Mary hugged me tightly. "You're a good kid, Aidan. You've just got to remember that."

"Thank you for everything." I was only beginning to realize how much I truly meant those words.

She gave me another hug, and we ate breakfast. Afterward, I excused myself. This time I didn't go to the beach or the cemetery. This time I took a different path to see where it would lead me. It led to a park, not with swings and kids, but with chessboards and people doing tai chi or yoga. This town had a lot more to explore than I originally thought.

I sat on a bench and watched the people around me. It was cooler than it had been our whole visit. Zipping my jacket, I took a deep breath of the fresh cool air. I caught sight of an old man sitting at one of the chess tables. He was alone, his head bowed. I waited for a few minutes to see if anyone would join him. No one did.

This was it.

This was my moment.

I tried to make my presence clear as I walked up to him. The last thing I needed was to startle the poor guy. "Excuse me, would you like to play a game?"

The man's eyes stayed on the board, he grunted, and his hands moved the pieces into place. Taking a seat, I moved my pawn. I didn't play chess often, but I could hold my own thanks to an old girlfriend. However, I could tell after only a few moves that this man's skills were levels above mine.

"Do you play chess a lot?" I asked.

Grunt.

We each took a few turns; I lost a pawn and a knight.

"It's beautiful here. Do you live nearby?"

Grunt.

"I'm only visiting. Mary—I don't know if you know her—she's my mom's aunt, but she's cool."

Grunt. And he took my castle.

I stopped trying to talk and focused on the game. I had a feeling my ex-girlfriend had led me to believe I'd been better than I really was. A few more moves and we were almost at checkmate. I stared at the board in deep concentration, trying to figure out how to save my king. It was pointless. He had already won ten moves ago.

I tipped the king over, surrendering. "Good game!" I reached my hand out to shake his, but he was already up and hobbling away.

Now it was my turn to grunt and run my hand through my hair in frustration. How did Annagale do this? What was her secret? How could I figure it out, and did I have enough time?

9

The Sun Comes Back

I was sitting on the beach when she returned. The sun was warm and the breeze cool, creating the perfect temperature. She was wearing a long bohemian skirt and a white tank top, a small box in her hand, and a huge grin on her face. Seeing her lifted my spirit like nothing else could. And yet I also felt despondent. I wanted her to tell me what was going on with her, yet I also wanted to live in ignorance. Sometimes ignorance was the safest place to be.

She knelt beside me and wrapped her arms around my neck. "I've missed you! How are you?" Pulling back, she stared into my face.

I likewise searched hers. Did she look more tired than normal?

"I'm glad you're back. How are you feeling?"

Turning her face to the sun, she spread her arms wide. "I. Am. Spectacular!" She took a long, deep breath. "What a glorious day it is! Perfect for our reunion. And we have cookies from my grandma to sweeten it." She handed me the small box.

Inside were indeed cookies, but I had no appetite.

Having her here, having her back, made the thought of losing her unbearable. "All you did was visit your grandma?" I forced the words out.

"Yup! She lives further in-state with a large, beautiful garden she tends to by herself. It's her pride and joy. My dad is slightly offended." She giggled at her joke; I could only stare intently at her.

"You didn't go or do anything else?"

"No, why?"

The next words came out in a rush; they had been building up all week. "Because I'm not ready to be you! I tried; I can't do what you do—not yet. I can't bring the joy you bring."

Her brow furrowed, and she grew still. I could see emotions flash across her face, but I couldn't pin down what she was thinking. Soon, she sank to the ground next to me. Still, she didn't say anything. The only noises around us were the crashing waves against the sand and the various random sounds of the other beachgoers.

When she spoke, her voice was contemplative. "Aidan, why would you want to be me?"

"You must see it—there's something magical about you, how you see things, how you live your life."

Her gaze shifted from me to the ocean. We sat in silence again as the minutes ticked by. She kept her gaze on the ocean as she spoke. "I'm never going to do anything great in life. Nothing big, nothing that would change the world. And I'm fine with that. But I do want to leave something behind. That's why I put the flowers out. My hope is someone will see them, and if they're having a bad day, that small flower might brighten it. Then, when they're having another bad day, they will remember that yellow flower and how it made them feel. I have to believe the small things we do have a much grander influence on the world than we think." She threaded her arm through mine and rested her head on my shoulder. "You will survive without me, Aidan. Humans are resilient beings. That's one of the things I love most about us."

I leaned my head against hers and closed my eyes, my heart beating erratically. The box of cookies lay next to us, forgotten.

10

Why Do You Have to Be Dying to Find Purpose in Life?

Annagale had been overjoyed at hearing what I had done while she was gone and the progress I had made with Mom. We decided to go to the park first thing in the morning so she could meet the old man and as she said see me "in action." The walk there was more enjoyable with her by my side, and I knew with her, the man would do more than grunt. But when we reached the park, Annagale spread a blanket under a tree and shooed me off to play the game.

The old man seemed grumpier today—his grunts were snippier, at least. My mind wasn't in it either and he had me in checkmate with only a few moves. Once done, he got up and shuffled away.

Shrugging, I made my way to Annagale. "See? He won't even talk to me. I don't think I'm doing any good. Probably the opposite; he's not spending as much time outside because once he's done with me, he leaves."

Annagale was sitting cross-legged, a notebook forgotten on her lap, her eyes distant as she absentmindedly tore at the grass.

"Annagale? Are you all right?"

She didn't face me, and her voice had the same contemplative tone it had had last night. "Why must someone be dying to find purpose in life? Isn't that awfully wasteful?"

My heart thumped hard against my chest. Here it was. Here was what I wanted. Answers. Why then did I wish I could run away? I forced myself to speak and tried to be calm. I needed to be strong for her. "I suppose because it makes us look at life, reminds us of how fragile it is."

I held my breath and waited for what I'd known was coming. Her next words were not what I expected.

When were they ever?

"Can we spend the day at your house? I would love to get to know your mom and aunt."

A stab of hurt kept me silent. Why wouldn't she just tell me?

However, I wanted her to *want* to tell me. "Sure, let's go." I folded the blanket, and we walked back home in silence.

Mom and Mary were happy to have company, especially since it was Annagale. They were more than a little curious about her, and how could I blame them?

Annagale did what she did best. The small, cozy house felt brighter and homier with her there. She asked Mary about the pictures and knickknacks on her mantel—why hadn't I done that? Mary's face lit up as she told us her stories.

It had been hard on her to never marry or have children, but she made the best she could of it. She tried to be close to her nieces and nephews; she smiled lovingly at Mom. And she had been blessed to have had a good job and few commitments, which allowed her to travel. She'd been to almost every continent.

"I loved traveling, but as the days passed, I wanted a bit of the world that was mine, a place where I could welcome other travelers. So, I bought this house, fixed it up, and tried to welcome everyone I could to it." This time, she grinned at me.

We moved out to the garden and helped pull weeds and plant flowers. Annagale kept up the stream of conversation with ease. I learned Mom had been going to school to become an engineer and left when she had gotten married. "No matter what's happened, I have no regrets marrying Chad and being a mom. I loved those years; they meant so much to me. But I wish I had finished my degree, now more than ever." She smiled warmly at me, and I knew she was afraid of hurting my feelings.

I smiled back. "I'll be going to college next year—maybe you should too?"

Again, I found myself wondering how I never knew any of this. Finally, admitted I was selfish, and not just since Dad left. I didn't appreciate life or what those around me had done and gone through in their own lives. What a waste.

****

Annagale stayed for dinner, and it was late by the time I walked her home. The coolness of yesterday was gone, and the heat of the day clung in the air.

Today had been near perfect. We walked slowly, not wanting it to end. During the evening, I had come to yet another realization. I debated whether I should tell her or not. Would she be mad? Happy? Feel the same way?

As we reached her house, I found the courage and pulled her to a stop beside me. "Do you think it's possible to love someone without being *in love* with them?" I smiled sheepishly. "I mean . . ." I took a breath, fully realizing how awkward I was making this, but I chose to blurt it out. "Annagale, I love you. You're like my best friend, like a sister."

Without a pause, she raised up on her tiptoes and kissed my cheek. "I know exactly how you feel. I love you too, Aidan."

My stomach unclenched, and a wave of joy rolled through me—and then dread. "Then tell me, are you dying? Do you have cancer or something?"

She tilted her head like she always did when she was deep in thought. "No. Aidan, you don't need to be dying to find life beautiful!"

11

I Don't Believe Her

"I don't believe you! Why won't you tell me the truth?"

She laughed. "I am telling you! I'm not sick. I'm not dying. What gave you the assumption I was?"

I paced away from her, my agitation growing. "People don't live like you! Life is hard, and it tears them down. They're selfish, lazy . . . They do stupid things that hurt others."

"I know." She stayed still as I paced, the beams of moonlight creating a gentle halo around her hair. Her voice was soft and pained. "I've seen how hard life can be for others. My life has been fairly easy so far, but I know it won't stay that way. I don't think it can."

Placing a hand on my arm, she stopped me mid-pace and

didn't speak until I looked at her.

"I'm hoping to store up joy and happiness. To be able to look back at my wonderful memories. To look back at the summer with Aidan. I want to hold on to these moments when life gets difficult. To remind myself of the good. It's all I can think to do."

We locked eyes as the seconds ticked by, the moon the only witness to her monumental announcement. My mind was stuck in a loop of one thought, finally it burst from my lips. "So, you're not dying?"

She shrugged. "Sorry?"

She was clearly laughing at me. I did not care. I needed a moment to fully process what that meant.

She wasn't dying.

She wasn't *dying*!

"I've been worried about you for weeks. Why didn't you tell me when I asked?"

She tossed her hands in the air with a look of mild exasperation. "Aidan, we had just met, you were clearly going through some stuff. And I did think you were a bit morbid. Plus, you haven't said anything about it since the first day we had lunch. Had I known you were truly worried, I would have given you a straight answer."

Bending over, I placed my hands on my knees, taking a deep breath.

"Aidan . . ."

I straightened and gave her a half-hearted smile. I grew even more aware of how much I genuinely, deeply, whole-heartedly, cared for her. She pulled me into a hug and held me close, as if she too were overcome with this encompassing love.

Did life work as she hoped? Could you store joy and happiness? I hoped so. I liked the idea. Mom had said something similar, how even with all the crap from Dad, she remembered the early days fondly. She held on to them.

What a huge relief it was to know Annagale wasn't going to die, at least not anytime soon. And there it was. We didn't know. No one did. Things could happen at any moment of any day. I had jumped to the assumption she was dying because she lived like she was.

She had been right on the first day we'd met—we were all dying. I held on tighter, grateful for the girl in my arms.

12

Culinary Expert

The next morning, I woke up feeling ecstatic. Knowing Annagale wasn't dying had removed a huge weight off my shoulders. Everything suddenly seemed okay with the world. To celebrate I was going to channel Annagale again; I was going to make today a good day.

Starting by doing something nice for Mom and Mary.

Why I decided I would make breakfast for them is still a mystery to me. I had never cooked before, and I hardly knew how to hold a spatula. But what better way to show my gratitude than by waking them with a blaring fire alarm? Mary came running down the stairs first. She caught me waving my arms in the air trying to clear the smoke, which now filled the room. I had tried to save the eggs from burning and had forgotten about the pancakes. Mom was only a few steps behind. When she saw me standing in the kitchen with one of Mary's aprons tied around my waist, a spoon in one hand and a look of horror on my face, she started laughing hysterically. The hold-your-stomach-can't-catch-your-breath kind of laughing. The type of laughter you can't help but laugh along with.

Once we calmed down, I untied the apron and flung it on the counter. "I'll clean this up, but first, I'm taking your Jeep. I'll be back."

As quick as I could, I drove to Teddy's and ordered three breakfast specials. When I got home, I found they'd not only *not* listened to me and had cleaned up my mess, but they also set the table.

I opened my mouth to complain, but Mom stopped me with a kiss on my cheek. "Before you go to college, you're learning to cook."

Laughing, I laid the food out, and we sat.

Mary grabbed a fork and opened her container. "You know, your mom used to make things out of her food before she would eat. She was very creative with it."

I smiled. "Yeah, she told me."

Mom looked embarrassed but also pleased.

"Annagale does something interesting when she eats too." I gestured to my plate. "She would take a bite of everything and decide what she'd want to eat last. She believes in living with intention, even with something as mundane as eating."

"She seems like a very sweet girl." Mom said.

I was glad she liked Annagale.

"Well, I'm old enough to eat whatever I want whenever I want, and I have a sweet tooth." Mary grabbed the syrup and generously spread it over her pancakes.

I chuckled and kept the conversation going. "You've traveled to so many places, I'm sure you've tried some interesting food. Do you have a favorite?"

Mary's eyes lit up like they did when Annagale had asked questions. Willingly, she shared story after story, full of laughter and heart. Not all were from her travels abroad. She said one of her most memorable meals was with her sister Kathy—my grandma. The sisters hadn't seen each other in months. Mary was leaving for a trip and would miss Thanksgiving.

"Thanksgiving had always been our favorite holiday. Kathy wanted to celebrate early so we could be together. I didn't expect much, but when I got there, the whole house was decorated for fall—this was in July, mind you. She was blasting the AC so we could wear our fall sweaters and drink cocoa. Oh, we had the best day! And the food! I have had many Thanksgivings, but none as good as that one."

Mom spoke, her eyes glistening with unshed tears. "I remember that. Mom talked about it all the time. It was one of her most cherished memories."

Now both had tears running down their cheeks.

Mom patted my hand. "Thank you, Aidan. This was wonderful."

"Yes, that Teddy sure knows how to make pancakes." Mary winked at me. "Now get going, boy. That sweet little friend of yours is probably waiting for you."

"No, it's okay, we'll have plenty of time together." It felt wonderful to say that. "I would like to spend time with the two of you, if that's okay?"

Mom turned her face away, and I knew she was crying again. We used to spend a lot of time together as a family, but after Dad's affair, I shut everyone out, furious it had all been a lie. Mom had never lied. Mom had always been there. I was also grateful to Mary; glad she had been there for Mom through everything.

Mary winked at me. "That would be nice. I would love to

show you around a bit. There are some pretty trails not too far away."

"Sounds great."

Mom wiped her eyes and turned back around. "Perfect!"

She grabbed her plate and stood. I stood as well and wrapped my arm around her shoulder. Neither of us said anything, but a lot was communicated in that one simple hug.

13

The Summer Nights Are Growing Shorter

"It's exhausting, you know, living like you do."

Annagale laughed. We were walking down the boardwalk; the heat of summer fading, and the smell of fall in the air.

"Not if you love it. It's the small things—smiling at someone, appreciating someone. It doesn't need to be big."

I nodded in agreement as I thought it through. It had been exhausting trying to be Annagale, but talking with Mom, learning more about Mary, those things hadn't been so difficult.

"Mom found some work in Boston. She thinks we may have found a decent apartment. I'll finish high school there and see what college I get into. Speaking of which, Mom got another call from my dad. He wants to pay for it."

"And are you letting him?"

"Mom and I talked it over, and yeah—it doesn't make what he did right, but it'll help. Finances are going to be tight."

Annagale threaded her arm through mine. "Aidan, I'm so happy for you. I know that decision must have been hard."

"What's hard is thinking about what I thought my life was going to be like before everything happened. Things are so different now. But I'm trying to make the best of it. Thanks to you."

"I think your life is going to be amazing Aidan! And I think you'll love Boston. And while I think it would've been fun to have gone through our last year of high school together, this way we will have to call and write letters."

"Write letters?"

"Yes, I love letter writing! It's nice to have something that takes more thought than a text, that takes time. Knowing a letter goes on its own journey from one person to the next, there's so much life in it. Don't you think?"

I moved my arm around her. "You are something else, Annagale."

She chuckled and leaned further into my side. "You know, this is my favorite part of a relationship. The middle. You begin to truly know the other person. Your actions and behavior change because of them, in a good way. The way in which it makes you a better person, because you're trying new things and thinking of someone else."

I kissed the top of her head, and we continued our walk as the sun set across the ocean.

****

Annagale and I spent the rest of the summer together as much as possible. We rented a tandem bike—which ended badly. I still have the scars. We visited the cemetery and the old man in the park. We went swimming, stargazing, and hiking. We read books in her backyard and watched our favorite movies together. Each moment felt special, perhaps because we knew it was coming to an end.

It was bittersweet.

We threw our families a barbecue, where we laughed, played card games, and talked about our futures. I felt freer than ever before; it was like the shattered pieces of my life were coming back together. It wouldn't look like it had before, and there would still be missing parts, but slowly it was forming into something that could be great.

With only a week left, we visited the cemetery again. I thought of asking where Annagale got the flowers, but decided I liked the mystery. Afterward, we went to the beach. Annagale made me promise not to move as she ran off and dug through the sand. She returned with two small seashells in her hands.

Her eyes were bright. "Are you ready?"

"For?" I took the shell she offered me.

"There's a legend that says if you whisper all your worries in a shell and throw them into the ocean the ocean gods will take them, hide them in their caverns, and return good fortune to you."

I looked at her with a raised eyebrow. "Sure, there is." Still, I followed her lead and held the shell in my hand close to my mouth; I whispered my worries, my anger, my pain, my fears, my disappointments, my insecurities, and the lost hope of what I thought my life would be.

Together we threw the shells as far as we could into the deep blue water.

Annagale tipped her head back. "Aidan, promise me you won't forget this summer. Promise me you'll write and call."

There was legitimate concern in her voice, and I wondered if she had needed me as much as I needed her.

"I promise, and I'll do one better. I'm coming back next summer! It's already planned."

A large smile spread across her face. "I'm glad you followed me to the cemetery that day."

So was I.

14

The Journey Back

Leaving Mary's was a vastly different experience from our arrival. I was sad to go.

And not just because I was leaving Annagale. I liked it there, and I liked Mary. I'd let go of so much anger and had rediscovered myself. Part of me was afraid leaving would change me for the worse. But Annagale had taught me each day was a choice. It sounds corny, but it's true. It was time to let go of my anger and to work on my hurt. I didn't know if I would ever have a relationship with my dad again. But I did know he wasn't going to hold me back anymore.

Mary hugged Mom tightly, both had tears in their eyes when they parted. It was a shame Mom hadn't found work here. They would have loved to live near each other, but there wasn't much work in a small town like this. Mary hugged me next, and I hugged her back.

"You're a good man. Don't forget! And you are welcome here anytime."

"Thank you, Mary."

Annagale was last. She hugged Mom and then me. We didn't say goodbye though. This wasn't goodbye; it was only the start.

****

On the drive to Mary's, I hadn't paid attention to anything. Now I did. I was blown away by how beautiful it all was. We had the ocean on one side and lush green trees on the other. Mom and I talked as well, we talked like we used to, and how we never had before. Both of us had changed through all of this, we had grown into something different, something maybe even better.

Dad hadn't quite given up on wanting custody, but I was old enough to make that choice, and with only a year left of high school, there was no point for him to fight what I wanted. Hopefully he would realize that and drop the issue.

I also learned more things about Mom. We had fixed the radio, and I played her some of my favorite, much more current stations. I realized she hummed along with every song—never sang, only hummed. Even to songs she didn't know. She also had an irrational fear that once the gas tank was less than half-full, we were going to run out. She said she didn't believe the gauges told the complete truth. To give her peace of mind, I made sure to keep my eye on it as well.

We rolled our windows down and basked in the wind and sun as we drove to our new home.

She grabbed my hand with her free one. "We're going to make it."

I squeezed back in agreement. I now believed we would.

15

The Next Steps and Fifteen Years Later

The apartment Mom and I found was far smaller than the home we had in the suburbs. But it was in a nice neighborhood close to the school and only a twenty-minute drive to Mom's work.

I would be lying if I didn't say school was difficult at first. I held on to the summer as much as I could—I went out of my way to talk to people. I tried out for track and other school activities— but being the new kid is a cliché for a reason. Every day I had to work on holding on to our summer, every day I had to remind myself to find the *moments*. Some days were better than others. Luckily Annagale was only a call away. By the end of the year, Mom and I had done well for ourselves in our new environment. And we did return the next summer and as many summers as we could after. Annagale and I stayed close throughout all the following years. We still write and call all the time.

She was right; trials did come her way. She wasn't accepted to her dream college, and for her first few terms, she struggled. Then during her junior year, her father got into an accident and developed an addiction to the painkillers he was prescribed. It was hard to be so far from her during those times. Our calls were even more frequent, we didn't often speak, but knowing I was there seemed to help.

We held on to the strength of each other and the knowledge that sunsets come but so do sunrises.

And we've both had some amazing sunrises.

I graduated college and am now a writer. I married the love of my life, and she had our first child a few months ago, a beautiful and healthy baby boy. Annagale is his godmother. I have a feeling he's going to be a very spoiled baby.

Annagale graduated college as well. She's a counselor now. Successful, although her methods can be unorthodox.

We live in different states but visit each other as often as we can. Our next visit will be her wedding. She met him, funny enough, playing chess. It's only natural she had better success than I did.

She just asked me to walk her down the aisle, to which I very gladly accepted.

I think that's what made me think of how this all started. How a hopeful girl helped a broken boy.

Life may not be all rainbows and sunrises, but they are there whenever we choose to look.

The summer with Annagale taught me that.

Acknowledgments

This story was created and written during a difficult period in my life. One of the things troubling me was the fear that my dream of publishing a book was foolish and would never happen. I had almost given up on writing as a whole.

But as I was lying in bed, unable to sleep, a name popped into my head – Annagale.

As soon as her name formed, her essence and the story unfolded. Frantically, I grabbed my phone and jotted down a chapter-by-chapter outline. Something like this has never happened before, and I doubt it'll happen again. Writing this book was therapeutic and it helped pull me out of some of my struggles. This book is very near and dear to my heart, and it is with excitement and trepidation that I share it with the world!

Before you go, let me share some Thank-yous. I believe in God, and I want to believe that He had a hand in not only my desire to be a writer, but in the creation of this book. Inspiration comes from somewhere - and I chose to believe it comes from Him.

Thank you to my critique partner, Hananya. Thank you for reaching out and asking if I wanted to swap stories. Thank you for helping me consistently work on my books. Thank you for your feedback, support, and friendship.

Thank you to my early readers, Ryn, Rebecca, Missy, and Claudia. Your feedback, excitement, and support mean the world to me! I am beyond grateful you took the time to read my book. Thank you for your suggestions, your phone calls of excitement, your sweet kind words, and your belief that *The Summer with Annagale* could be a help to others.

A huge thank you to Alicen. Alicen has always been the first to read my writing. She has heard me talk endlessly about my stories for years! She's been a sounding board and a support when I felt like I was failing and there was no chance of me living my dream. This book and I would not be here without her!

A shoutout to my editors: Writerverse and Enchanted Ink Publishing. Thank you for taking my story and making it better!

And finally, I want to thank you - the reader! Without you my dream would stop with me hitting publish. But you have brought new and different life into this book. Thank you for taking a chance and picking up *The Summer with Annagale*.

It helped me and gave me a glimmer of hope when I needed it, I hope it can do the same for you!

About the Author

Colleen Smith has always wanted to be an author, publishing her debut novel in 2023 was a dream come true. She is a multi-genre writer and doesn't like to be put into a box – just try and get her to answer what her favorite *anything* is. When she isn't writing she's trying to figure out life and stay sane while doing it–so far, most days she's succeeding.

Book discussion questions

i. At the beginning of the story Aidan is feeling lost and confused. He projects this by being angry and wanting to be alone. How have you dealt with similar issues?

ii. Aidan feels more hopeful after his first encounter with Annagale. This happened, of all places in a cemetery. Have you ever found hope in unconventional places?

iii. Both Aidan and Annagale had moments in their life when they lost hope. How do you nurture hope when things are difficult?

iv. Aidan jumps to a quick conclusion about

Annagale because of how she lives her life. Have you ever jumped to conclusions about others? Was it a positive or negative experience? What conclusions do you think people would jump too about you?

v.   Annagale loves to take ordinary things and make them extraordinary. In what small ways could you add a little extraordinary in your daily life?

vi.   Annagale believes that any moment could be 'a moment'. How can we be more present to soak up these potential memory making moments?

vii.   Aidan struggled trying to be like Annagale until he discovered he only needed to be himself. What passions/gifts/talents do you have that could help those around you?

viii.   Annagale wants to leave her mark on the world, even in small ways. What ways can you leave a positive mark on the world?

ix.   When Aidan tried to help the older man by playing chess, he didn't feel like he succeeded. Do you think he did? What do you think we should do when our efforts don't seem to be doing anything?

x.   Annagale wants to save up the good moments in life to hold onto when life gets difficult. Do you think that is possible?

xi.   Aidan believes sunsets represent the low moments in our lives—when darkness takes over. What are your thoughts about sunsets?

xii.   If you were to paint your version of a sunset, what would it look like?

xiii.   Do you think we can live like we're dying? Should we?

xiv.   Aidan realizes that his mother, like himself, is only human. Has there been a time that you've realized the same thing about a parent or someone you look up to? How did that affect you?

xv. We never see Aidan forgive his father. Do you think it was wrong of him not to?

xvi. Hope is a major theme in this book. How would you describe hope?

THANK YOU!

Thank you for reading *The Summer with Annagale*. If you enjoyed this book, please leave a review at Amazon or your vendor of choice. Reviews help authors so much!

Follow me on Instagram for writing/reading updates and cute pictures of my dog, @colleensmithwrites or scan the QR code.

Where is Annagale?

Help me follow Annagale around the world! Email whereisannagale@gmail.com with your name and city/state/country you live in along with any thoughts you would like to share. I would love to hear from you!

You can also use the hashtag #whereisannagale when posting about *The Summer with Annagale* on social media and see what others are saying!

I'm excited to see the places Annagale and Aidan will reach!

Disclaimer: please remember to be safe online! Be careful where you share personal information. I will never share any information without written consent.

www.ingramcontent.com/pod-product-compliance
Lightning Source LLC
Chambersburg PA
CBHW031414310726
48971CB00003B/857